A
Thousand
and One
Chickens

A
Thousand
and One
Chickens

Seymour Rossel

Illustrated by
Vlad Guzner

UAHC PRESS · NEW YORK

Library of Congress Cataloging-in Publication Data

Rossel, Seymour.
   A thousand and one chickens / Seymour Rossel ; illustrated by
Vlad Guzner.
      p.   cm.
   Summary: An arrogant king precipitates a situation whose
solution brings together an ordinary family and a royal family from this
small Jewish town of Chelm.
   ISBN 0-8074-0541-8
   [1. Jews—Poland—Folklore.   2. Chelm (Chelm, Poland)—
Folklore.
3. Folklore—Poland.]   I. Guzner, Vlad, ill.   II. Title.
PZ8.1.R695Th 1995
398.2'089924—dc20
[E]   95-32230
                                                          CIP
                                                           AC

For my brother
C A R Y

Not only did he share his wisdom
with his many children,
he made many children his own
by his years of teaching
in the religious school
—*Seymour Rossel*

To my mother
—*Vlad Guzner*

A Word about Chelm

In the Talmud, the sage Ben Zoma taught:

Who is wise? The person who learns from all people . . . Who is strong? The person with self-control . . . Who is rich? The one who is happy with his or her lot . . . Who is honored? The one who honors others.

To this we might add, "Who is happy? The one who smiles and causes others to smile."

For generations our people have loved hearing the fabulous stories of the so-called "wise" citizens of the imaginary city of Chelm.

It is said that Chelm was once just an ordinary town, much like the one you live in. One day a kindly angel thought, "The world would be a happier place if the few foolish souls scattered here and there were replaced with wise souls." So the angel grabbed a huge bag of wise souls from heaven and threw the bag over his shoulder. He went from town to town trading a wise soul from the bag for each foolish soul he could find.

At long last there were no foolish souls left anywhere in the world. They were all in the angel's bag. As he started to fly back to heaven, the angel was very pleased with himself. Just then a gust of wind swept the bag from his hands, and the foolish souls spilled onto a mountaintop.

Before the angel could collect them, all the foolish souls rolled down the mountain into a sleepy little town and entered the people who lived there. The angel followed the souls into the town, but when he got there, he discovered an extraordinary thing.

In every other town he visited, the people had been happier when their foolish souls had been traded for wise ones. But here all the foolish souls seemed very happy living together. Everyone smiled, and the town was filled with laughter.

In the end, the angel flew back to heaven, leaving the foolish souls to their merry ways. Chelm was the name of the town at the bottom of the mountain. Ever since, Chelm has brought joy to Jews young and old. Stories of the people of Chelm multiplied through the ages. The stories had much in common: Each told how the people of Chelm tackled their problems with foolish solutions and how every foolish solution seemed to have just a little wisdom in it, after all.

This book tries to imagine what the world might have been like if Chelm had been an entire kingdom. I hope you will have some fun reading it aloud; and don't be too surprised if the foolishness that makes you laugh also makes you think.

—Seymour Rossel

CHAPTER ONE

The Sages Three

Once, long ago, in a small town at the very edge of the kingdom of Chelm, there lived three sages of great fame. One was celebrated as the first man ever to knit his brow. Ideas seemed always lurking just behind his wrinkled forehead. And, in his Academy of Forehead Knitting, many a young boy or girl sat six long hours each day flexing eyebrow muscles and scrunching up skin.

The second sage was the inventor of "Aha!" In the stillness of the night, when birds had stopped chirping and the creatures of the daytime were silent, when the sages were all tucked in beneath their blanket, this sage would suddenly sit bolt upright in bed, raise one finger high, and exclaim, "Aha!"

The dog would yap in fear. The cat would startle, hump her back, and hiss like a smoldering coal struck by water. In the distance, a wolf would howl at the moon, and alarmed frogs would croak warnings to the pond.

The sage would leap from bed (pulling the covers with him), stand in the middle of the room, put one finger upon his chin, and repeat—more distinctly—"Aha!"

Who could sleep with such a hullabaloo going on? His brother sages rose from the mattress, donned their robes, and warmed themselves by the fireplace. The mongrel dog scurried under the bed and hid. The cat sat stiff and alert. Then, just as stillness returned, the second sage raised one leg. Deliberately, he struck the floor with his foot, and the noise echoed as again he shouted the single word "Aha!"

No doubt about it. Something had gotten into him! Neighbors, awakened in the middle of the night, heard the "Aha!" and turned sleepily to wives and husbands. "The sage has a new idea. What a wise man! It's his third idea this week."

For a while, the sage would remain poised, his finger still resting upon his chin. Then he began to whisper to himself. And if you listened carefully, you could hear him repeating in a very low voice, "Aha, aha, aha, aha, aha . . ."

Over and again he muttered his word. He whispered it as he crawled into bed. He muttered it as the other two sages settled down beneath the blanket again. He babbled it as the dog sniffed the air, placed its tongue between its teeth, rested its head on its crossed forepaws, and set to snoring. He murmured it as the cat curled up on the rug beside the hearth. He uttered it beneath his breath as the night grew calm. He said it this way and that: "Aha?" and "Aha . . ." and "Aha!"

He mumbled it softly until even he fell asleep to the sound of "aha, aha, aha, aha."

When at last all was still—when the last "aha" faded in a lonely sounding "ah," an owl, perched in the tree outside the sages' window, answered, "Hoo."

So, it was brow-knitting that made the first

sage famous. And it was "aha"-ing that made the second sage famous. But the third sage was the most famed of all. He was known far and wide, from Chelm's hither to Chelm's yon and back, for that most wondrous invention of wisdom: the ponder.

Ensconced in his chair from dawn to dusk, he cupped his head in his hands and pondered. First he pondered the wooden table as if it would sprout branches and leaves. Then he pondered the wall, looking at it from top to bottom and corner to corner, tilting his head this way and that, as if expecting the wall to tilt, too. He pondered his food, pushing the peas from one side of his plate to the other, rolling them on their shrunken-up edges, as if to ask, "What makes peas shrivel up that way when they are boiled?"

At times he pondered the first sage's wrinkled brow. He came up close to the master of furrows and leaned over precariously, nearly colliding with the sage's face. Then he fixed his gaze on a wrinkle or two and pondered as if studying a timberline along the ridges of the sage's forehead or rivers flowing in dry wrinkled valleys.

At times the third sage pondered with his ears.

He perked up one ear, holding it higher than the other, placing his finger before his lips to request silence, and listening intently. Then, if the dog barked or the cat meowed, he paced up and down the floor, yelling, "Can't you see I'm pondering? Can't you see I'm pondering? You must be quiet! You must be quiet!"

Of course, the best pondering with ears was done when the second sage suddenly raised a finger in the air and cried, "Aha!" The third sage would set himself squarely beside the second, tilt one ear toward the second sage's mouth, and ponder deep and hard. Soon came the next "Aha!" and the next after that. Then came the many, many whispered "aha"s that had made the second sage so famous. And the third sage would nod his head this way and shake his head that way and say, "I told you so. Didn't I tell you so?"

And that was how they lived. One sage, two sages, three sages. Wrinkling the brow, yelling "Aha!" and pondering.

The townspeople arose at dawn and went out to milk the cows. Some kneaded bread. Some baked it. Some carried the water, and others split

logs for the fireplace. Some grew corn, some grew wheat. Some sat by the river, catching fish. Some went hunting in the forest. They raised children. They raised sheep. They raised chickens. But the three sages did none of these. Wrinkling the brow, crying "Aha!" and pondering—such were their vocations.

Naturally someone had to be found to look after them—to milk their cow and bake their bread, to stoke their fire and feed their dog and cat, to wash their clothing and change the linens on their bed. And so the search began.

CHAPTER TWO

The Woodsman's Wife and Daughters Three

On the edge of town lived a woodsman, his wife, and his daughters. The woodsman's name was Jacob, and his wife's name was Rebecca. But since people often find it a bother to call others by long and lovely sounding names, the neighbors called Rebecca by the simpler name "Becky." And Jacob, they just called "Jake."

Whether a hot summer dawn or a cold winter morn, Jake woke up to the rooster's cacophonous crow. After a breakfast of tea, cheese, and bread, he placed his ax across his shoulder and threaded his way through the woods, greeting the oak, the elm, and the walnut, the maple, the willow, and the pine.

Though his livelihood came from chopping down trees and sawing them into building boards or splitting them into firewood, Jake was a friend to the forest. He never cut young trees, for they gave the forest new life. And he never cut ancient trees, for they provided shade to the forest floor, and their hollows were home to the small animals.

Jake took down only the large trees crowded together, blocking the sunlight so that the small trees could not grow. And that, as everyone knows, is what makes a good woodsman good.

Jake had three daughters. The oldest was Deborah, the next was Amelia, and the youngest was Blossom. People called Deborah "Deb." Amelia they called "Amy." As for Blossom, well, they just called Blossom "Blossom."

From the beginning, Blossom seemed different from other girls. When she cried for the first time, it was a cry so piercing and sad that even her mother could not bear to hear it. The frightened midwife placed the newborn in Becky's arms, but still that strange and fearsome shriek persisted.

The women of the town each took a turn holding Blossom, trying to quiet the newborn. But the more they sang to her, the more they cuddled her, the more they rocked her, the more they tickled her chin, and the more they cooed in her face, the more the baby screamed. Only in her father's arms did Blossom stop crying, curl up, and fall fast asleep.

Morning, evening, and night, Becky sobbed, her head in her hands. Deb and Amy took turns bringing towels to their mother, drying her eyes, wiping her cheeks. But Becky never stopped weeping. "My baby does not love me," she cried.

The neighbors were puzzled. Such a thing had never happened before. Could it be that a baby would not cling to its mother? Could it be that a mother was unable to comfort her own child? So it seemed. For whenever Becky reached into the crib to pick Blossom up, the baby would begin her same awful shriek. Blossom cried and cried until Jake came home and held her.

So it came to pass that one spring day, just before Passover, Becky kissed her three girls and

told Deb and Amy, "Take good care of your father and your little sister." Tearfully, Becky then put a few things in a small sack, tied the sack to the end of a stick, and walked out the door.

Deb and Amy obeyed their mother. Early each morning, they milked the cow and fed the chickens. The girls baked bread and prepared the meals. They sang lullabies to their baby sister, changed her diapers, and held her close. Blossom cried no more.

*F*or a long time, Jake was sad. He sat up late at night and listened, hoping to hear Becky's footsteps. Once he flung open the door at midnight, fully expecting Becky to be standing there. But Becky did not return. After that, he forced himself to listen no more.

Deb grew tall and strong. When she could fit into the dresses her mother had left behind, Deb kissed Amy and Blossom and said, "Take good care of father." She put a few things in a sack, tied the sack to the end of a stick, and walked out the door.

Amy soon did the same. Kissing and hugging Blossom she said, "Promise me you'll milk the cow and feed the chickens and bake the bread and make the meals." Blossom promised. Then Amy packed her clothing in a sack and tied the sack to a stick and walked from the house, never looking back. And so it came to pass that Jake and Blossom lived together in the small house at the edge of town.

Blossom grew strong and tall. But, unlike her sisters, Blossom did not leave home. Every day she rose to the rooster's call, milked the cow, fed the chickens, baked the bread, cooked the meals, and sang the songs her sisters had taught her. And every afternoon, when the chores were done, Blossom ran to the forest to find her father.

Jake taught Blossom the names of all the trees and the animals of the woods. He showed her which mushrooms and bush berries were good to eat and which herbs could be used for tea and which spices were best to flavor meats and salads for Shabbat. In time, Blossom came to know the forest as well as did her woodsman father.

In the evenings, Jake read to Blossom by candlelight. Together they read all the stories of the

Bible. And when they had finished the Bible, they read stories of kings and queens, princes and princesses, dragons and knights, enchanted forests and ships that sailed wherever the four winds blew.

As she fell asleep, Blossom dreamed of living in Solomon's palace, of riding white horses, of wandering through the wilderness, and of sleeping in feather beds. On the way to market each week, she imagined herself royally striding along pathways of flowers leading from the Temple in Jerusalem to the center of Chelm.

The women of the town shook their heads and clucked their tongues as if to say, "There is something very wrong with this girl." If the women had thought deeply, they might have said, "There is something *special* about this girl." But, of course, no one in the kingdom of Chelm thought too deeply.

𝒟eb was the first to come home. She appeared one day in the doorway as Jake and Blossom sat reading from the Bible. And, standing behind her—a wide-brimmed hat held tightly in his hands—was a young man. He was big and handsome, with a shock of yellow hair as mismanaged as the edges of the sun. Deb kissed her father and said, "This is my husband. He wants to be a woodsman." Pleased with the fine boy, Jake promised to teach the blond-haired youth everything there was to know about being a woodsman. Then Deb kissed Blossom and said, "I have come home again. For in all the world there is no better place than home."

It could not have been more than three years later—it could not have been four—when Amy knocked on the door. Blossom ran to open it and found her second sister standing there—a young man by her side. He was shorter than Deb's husband, but every bit as handsome. His dark hair was the color of a hazelnut, and his hands were as rough as the bark of a maple tree. "This is my husband," Amy announced. "He's a carpenter and a builder of houses." Jake wept to see what a fine man his daughter had chosen for a husband. "Come in," he said, "and make this your home. You are welcome here." They entered the house and never again left the family.

It could not have been six months later—it could not have been seven—when there came another knock. Jake rushed to open the door, his heart nearly jumping from his chest. He threw his arms about Becky, then stood back to examine her from head to foot. "The years have been good to you," he said at last. "You are even more beautiful now than you were on the day you left." She laughed the tingling laugh he had not heard since the day Blossom was born. "I have traveled many a mile," she said and sighed.

Becky saw Deb sitting by the fireplace and ran to kiss her. Then she embraced Amy. There were kisses for the two young men—the tall blond one and the shorter dark one.

All the while, Blossom stood in the shadows by the table. At last, her mother turned to her and smiled. Then she laughed, and, for the first time anyone could remember, Blossom laughed, too.

CHAPTER THREE

Work for Wisdom— Blossom Finds a Job

Blossom was the most beautiful of the three sisters. Her raven-black hair, thick and silken, reached in its braided length to the middle of her back. Her eyes were sapphire gems and her cheeks the color of a delicate rose. Still, none of the young men of the town courted her.

Blossom spent her time talking with her sisters and listening to the stories her mother told of the world beyond the woods. She ate lunch in the forest with her father. She sat for hours reading to herself the tales of knights, princes, and kings.

The neighbors said, "She is growing old, you know. And beauty passes quickly."

One Sabbath eve, her father came home from the forest and drew her aside. "There is not enough work for you here at home," he said. "But I have heard of a job not far away."

Blossom took hold of her father's hand. "I am happy here," she said. "And I am busy all the day."

"That is true," her father answered. "But being busy is hardly the same as working. I think you will like this job."

He told her of the three wise men who lived together in a house in town. One, he said, was the inventor of the wrinkled brow. The second was the very man who had discovered "Aha!"— and "Aha!" was easily the most important word of wisdom ever spoken, at least since the time that "Eureka!" had been uttered. And as famous as both of the other sages put together was the third sage, who had chanced upon the art of pondering.

"The time has come," her father said to Blossom, "for you to stop studying the ways of the forest and to stop reading books that tell nothing of the world as it truly is. You must go and learn the wisdom of Chelm. These three sages can teach you much if you pay close attention and serve them as you have served me."

Soon it was arranged. Blossom went to work for the sages. She rose each morning to leave her father's house, entered the town, and made her way to the sages' rickety cabin. She cooked for them. She did their laundry and tended their fire. She carried water for them from the well, baked their bread, and sewed patches on their threadbare trousers. She milked the cow and fed the chickens and tended the dog and the cat. On Shabbat, she lit the candles that warmed the sages' hearts.

In return, they gave her lessons. The first sage revealed to her many of the deepest secrets of knitting the forehead. "Just so," he would say, forcing her eyebrows ever closer to her bangs with his fingers; or "Like this," he would say, pulling her ears sharply in the direction of her nose. And though he was as patient as a teacher could be, Blossom could not keep a wrinkle in her brow.

The second sage gave her lessons in the art of

the proper "Aha!" He made her practice by the hour, showing her just how to drop her chin, how to take in a long breath and release it all at once with a force that landed on the "ah" and echoed in the "ha!" He smiled when she did it well but frowned when she asked, "How will I know *when* to say it?"

Always he answered, "That must come from within. You will know when the perfect moment comes." But, try as she might, the perfect moment never seemed to come. Many a time she watched as this sage jumped to his feet and cried out his wondrous motto. Many a time she saw him raise one leg in the air and stamp at the floorboards with all his might, crying simultaneously at the top of his lungs, "Aha!" Yet Blossom never felt an urge to say it, and all her practice came to naught.

Watching all this, the third sage said, "It is no wonder the two of you have failed. The girl is a born ponderer. I will teach her how to ponder."

So he set about giving Blossom instruction in "The Finer Points of Ponder." He showed her how to strum the tabletop with her fingertips, how to tilt her head and perk up one ear to listen, how to sit motionless for an hour at a time, and how to observe closely things that did not move.

Once he made her stare for an entire afternoon at a half-filled glass of tea. Just when she thought she could bear no more, he asked, "Well?" And she answered, "Well."

And he asked, "Well?"

And she answered, "Well."

And he snorted, "Well!" with a huff and stormed away from her, pacing back and forth across the room with his hands clasped tightly behind his back. Then he turned to her again and said, "Well, well, well."

And she knew he was not pleased.

*T*he three sages held a meeting to decide what should be done. "Not a ponderer at all," said the ponderer. "And not a forehead knitter, either," said the sage of the furrowed brow. "And certainly not very bright when it comes to 'Aha!' " said the third. "What shall we do with the girl?" they asked.

"On the other hand, we must not lose her," the first sage said. "She bakes challah that tastes like cake." The second sage agreed. "No one makes a finer chicken soup," said he. And the third one added, "By all means, we must keep her. Look at the linens on the bed—they're clean. We have fresh eggs and milk every day. The dog and the cat have never been so well fed. And she makes every Sabbath and holy day special."

So it was settled. The lessons came to an end. And, from time to time, the three sages gave Blossom a gold coin or a silver one, or a few copper coins they earned by teaching students or judging a case or settling an argument—such are the things wise men are paid for. And Blossom went right on working for them.

Blossom was glad not to have the lessons. Her brow had begun to ache from all the wrinkling. Her voice had become hoarse from practicing "Aha!" And she had certainly had her fill of staring at things that did not move. She began to question whether these three men were really as wise as the people of Chelm claimed.

Blossom did not doubt that pondering was a great invention. Who could doubt it? And she loved to hear the sound of "Aha!" righteously uttered. Who would not? And she thought that anyone with a brow as wrinkled as that of the Forehead Knitter had to be wise beyond compare. For who could possibly believe otherwise? Nevertheless, she doubted.

Then, one day, late in autumn, her moments of doubt came to an end. A man and wife came to the rickety cabin and begged the sages to save their marriage.

The man was a tailor who worked all day at home. While shortening cuffs, he sang a song. While stitching and mending, he sang a song. While sewing and basting, he sang a song. Singing and working were one and the same to him, he said. And all three of the wise men smiled. "What could possibly be the problem?" they asked.

"Ayee!" the woman cried. "This man of mine is driving me out of my wits! He knows but one song. He sings it all day long. He sings it while shortening and hemming, sewing and basting, stitching and mending. The same song! And worse, it is not even a pleasant song!"

"And *you?*" the tailor asked accusingly of his

wife. "All day long you gossip. A woman comes into the house with a pair of trousers to be mended, and all the while I am working, you are talking. A man brings me his best suit to let out, and all the while I am opening seams, you are gabbing. Why, even when there is no one else around, you talk. You gossip. You nag. You pit and you patter. You wig and you wag. There is no end to your prattle."

"I talk because your song is driving me crazy," the woman said.

"And I sing because your chatter makes me ill," the man replied.

The two argued back and forth before the sages, filling the cabin with the brittle noise of anger. The man called gossip devil's talk. The woman said the tailor's tune was a witch's curse.

Suddenly, the man and the woman stopped arguing and turned to the sages. "You see," the woman said, "you must tell us what can be done. For I truly love this half-witted tailor, and I do not wish to leave him."

And the tailor said, "Yes, tell us what must be done. For I truly love this yakkety woman, and I could not do without her."

Then the sages did what sages do. The first one tightly knitted his brow. He clenched his fists and fixed the wrinkles in his forehead steady and deep. Not a moment passed before the second sage rose up and yelled out an "Aha!" that startled the dog. This was followed by another "Aha!" and after that a long, low series of "aha"s that became ever softer until they could not be heard. Meanwhile, the third sage was pondering the ceiling, his head tilted upward, studying each beam and board above.

As Blossom watched, thinking, "Nothing can possibly come of all this," the room grew still. It seemed as if the air itself were a vessel waiting to be broken. A minute passed, then another, and another. The room remained silent. Blossom wondered for an instant if *anything* would ever happen again.

Suddenly the tailor and his wife smiled at each other.

"I am so glad that we came," said the woman. "They said these three men were wise—but I never imagined that any men could be *this* wise!"

"Yes," agreed the tailor. Then he addressed the sages. "We will never forget your wisdom.

For you have saved our marriage. Silence is the perfect answer."

"From now on," said the woman, "I shall be quiet while my husband is working—as quiet as quiet can be—for talking can certainly be stopped."

"From now on," said the tailor, "I shall always be silent while I work—as silent as a needle slipping through cloth—for singing can certainly be stopped."

Then the tailor kissed his wife, thanked the three sages again, left a purseful of coins upon the table, and together the couple danced out the door.

Blossom watched to see what would happen next. The three sages stayed precisely as they were—brow knit, finger in air, and face turned up to the ceiling.

At long last, Blossom began to whistle one of her father's tunes. She took the feather duster and swept a cobweb from one corner of the room. Looking at the three motionless sages, she shook her head and laughed to think how any solution so simple could be so wise.

CHAPTER FOUR

A Most Royal Problem

Far away, in the capital city of the kingdom of Chelm, the king sat in his chair, wondering why thrones had to be so uncomfortable, why crowns had to be so heavy, and why robes of velvet with braids of gold had to be so stuffy. He was a most uncomfortable king. He did not like being king at all. In fact, what he had always wanted to be was a jester, but instead, he was the king of Chelm.

He loved jokes. He reveled in funny stories that made people laugh. He wished that every day could be Purim. He imagined himself dancing merry jigs across the marble floor, stumbling and shuffling, nearly falling with every twist and turn. He adored singing a song off-key or turning up his nose and sniffing the air as the queen did when she spoke.

Once in a while he played at being a jester. Every time he made up a funny story and told it to the gentlemen and ladies of the court, they clapped gently, but when the story came to its silly conclusion, no one laughed. Instead, every gentleman turned to his lady and gave her a quizzical look.

Once the king did a jesterly dance for the court. He tipped this way and that. He stumbled and quite nearly fell flat on his nose. He turned a neat pirouette and came down with a smack on the floor, landing on his bottom with a royal thud. Then he turned up his face with a smile and waited to hear laughter. But the ladies of the court covered their faces with their fans, embarrassed to see a king flat on his behind. And the gentlemen turned their faces away, just to be polite.

The queen scolded her husband and made him

promise to walk more carefully in the future. Turning her nose in the air, she said, "You will surely hurt yourself." "I suppose you are right," the king sighed, and he sent scouts to find the best jester in the kingdom. After searching near and far, the scouts chose a lad from a small town at the very edge of the kingdom of Chelm.

Dressed in a patchwork suit of green and red silk, bright yellow shoes that curled up at the toes, and a conical hat with a tiny brass bell, the jester brought mirth to the palace. The stories he told made the court echo with laughter, the dances he danced made the ladies giggle with glee, and so merry were the songs he sang that the gentlemen jumped up and down like circus poodles.

Even the queen would at times bring down her nose to assign a royal chuckle to the jester. The jester's success made the king jealous. The king frowned when the jester made others laugh, and he looked away when the jester juggled. The more the queen and prince enjoyed the jester's antics, the more somber and sullen was the king.

The king was like a spoiled child who had

chosen a toy and wished he had chosen another. Something awful was bound to happen.

One day the king grew very hungry. He was judging at the time, settled on his throne, attempting to appear regal in his crown and robes. He turned to his son, the prince, and said, "Be a good boy. Run to the kitchen to fetch me six eggs to eat. Bring them whole and bring them fast." "Right away," said the prince, running off to the kitchen.

On the way to the kitchen the prince ran down a very long hall. Suddenly the jester appeared and placed himself squarely in the way. Acting like a royal guard, the jester cried out, "Halt! Who goes there?"

"No time for fun," said the prince. "I'm running to the kitchen to fetch my father a snack. Six eggs he wants. Whole and fast."

"Allow me," said the jester, and he, too, began to run. They reached the kitchen together, both out of breath.

"What is it?" asked the cook, surprised. "Do

we have unexpected company for dinner? A visiting duchess, perhaps? A wise old rabbi with mystic tales to tell? A knight with many horsemen to feed?"

"Nothing of the sort," said the jester.

"No," said the prince. "My father wishes a snack. Six eggs for the king. And he wants them whole, and he wants them fast."

It was not the cook's first day on the job. He knew well what the king liked to eat, and he always kept plenty on hand. Rushing to a pot that stood on the stove, he pulled out six eggs, peeled them, placed the eggs on a silver platter, and handed the platter to the prince. "Six eggs," he said, "as fast and as whole as can be. But, mind, hold the platter carefully for eggs are slippery."

The prince thanked the cook and set off again on the run. Clapping his hands and leaping up in the air, the jester took off after the prince.

You can imagine what happened next. The prince was running and the eggs were sliding and the hall was long and—look out! Halfway down the hall, one egg slipped from the tray, rolled down the prince's arm, and landed on the floor, *kerplop!*

"Ho, ho!" said the jester, stopping to pick up the fallen egg. "No king would eat an egg that has fallen from grace. So let me just show you a trick. Have you ever seen a man make an egg disappear?"

"No, never," said the prince, hardly thinking.

And with one sudden movement, the jester wiped the egg on his red and green silk suit and plopped it into his mouth. A few quick chews and the egg was gone. "There," he said to the prince. "a clean end to a dirty egg." And the boy and the jester laughed.

"Oh, my heavens," said the prince, "the king is still waiting for his snack." And he set off again. The jester paused in the middle of the hall to take a small bow to no one in particular, then ran after the prince. And that was how they entered the throne room, still running, five eggs swooshing about the silver tray.

"Ah, what have we here?" said the king with a grin. "My snack in a flash." And he reached out a hand to pick up an egg.

Then a look of horror passed over his face. His hand halted in midair. Pointing one finger, the king started to count. "One. Two. Three. Four.

Five." Then he looked at the prince. "Did I not ask for *six* eggs? Where is egg number six?"

The prince shrugged his shoulders and turned to look at the jester. The jester shrugged his shoulders and turned to look behind him. And, since there was no one behind the jester, all the gentlemen and ladies of the court laughed.

The king, however, was not amused. He counted again: "One. Two. Three. Four. Five. What happened to egg number six?" he demanded.

Bowing deeply, the jester replied, "Five eggs for a hungry king—and one for a flea-bitten jester. I have made one egg disappear."

"Nay," said the king. "You have stolen what belongs to the king of Chelm. And you shall pay. You shall pay very dearly indeed. For you have not stolen a mere egg. You have stolen nearly half my kingdom!"

"No," said the gentlemen of the court, covering their open mouths in horror. "Can it be?" asked the ladies.

"Indeed," repeated the king, turning up his nose in the manner of the queen at her worst. "An egg is an enormous thing to steal. From one

egg hatches one chicken. And from one chicken may come dozens of eggs. And from each of those eggs another chicken. And each of those dozens of chickens may hatch dozens of eggs more, each of which hatches still another chicken. And, therefore," concluded the king, "you have stolen not *one egg,* you lowly jester. You have stolen *a thousand and one chickens* from the king's treasury!"

"No," said the gentlemen of the court, covering their mouths. "It is so," said the ladies of the court, folding their fans.

"Now," said the king in his most lordly manner, "can you pay me the cost of a thousand and one chickens?" The jester shook his head, causing the little bells atop his cap to jingle.

"Just as I thought," the king said sternly. "Then, in all fairness, I must ask you please for your head." The king then called for the executioner. The lords and ladies of the court were sad. There was no laughter now. The executioner entered the room, his glistening steel sword in his hand. "Bend over, if you will," he said to the jester, "and would you be so kind as to stick out your neck, just to make my job a little easier?"

"Wait!" cried the prince. "This is all my fault. For I dropped the egg while I was running. It slid from the silver platter and landed on the floor. If anyone should lose his head, let it be me!"

"No!" cried the king. "This is terrible."

It was clear to one and all—to every gentleman and every lady of the court, to the king and the queen, and to the executioner as well—that it was indeed the prince's fault, and the prince would have to pay. For it was he who had dropped the egg and made it unfit for a king to eat.

"Forget the whole thing," said the king.

$\mathcal{T}$he executioner cleared his throat and said, "Please forgive me for saying this, Your Majesty, but a royal verdict must be carried out, for that is *your* law."

"No!" gasped the gentlemen and ladies of the

court. "Oh, my dear," cried the queen, dropping to the floor in a faint.

When at last the queen was roused, the king turned sadly to the executioner and said, "If the sword is sharp, it must be done."

The prince kneeled and stretched his neck over the king's footstool. The executioner raised his sword high into the air and took aim. But just as the fatal blow was about to fall, a single voice cried out, "Wait!" All eyes turned to the jester. "There may yet be a way to save the prince," he said.

The king ordered the executioner to step back and lower his sword. "Speak up, Jester," said the king. "How can we save the prince?"

"I come from a small town at the very edge of the kingdom," said the jester, "a town that is famous for its three sages. Together, they are the wisest men in all Chelm.

"Surely, these three sages can solve the problem. They can tell us how to save the life of the prince so that we might live happily ever after."

"Very well," said the king, with a wave of his hand. "Send for the three sages."

"Oh, dear me, no," said the queen. "That will

take too long. First, you will have to send some-
body many miles to find them. Then, they will
have to journey many miles back. I do not think
I can bear to wait so long."

"Very well," said the king with a royal frown.
He turned to his court and proclaimed, "Let everyone prepare. For when the sun rises tomor-
row, we depart."

CHAPTER FIVE

Journey to Wisdom

W hat a fabulous parade! It was like Sim-
chat Torah without the apples. There
were flag carriers and trumpeters. Gentlemen on
their horses. Ladies on their ponies. Dogs
aplenty, yapping and barking at the horses'
hooves, urging them on. At the head of the line
rode the king astride his all-white stallion; behind him, the queen in her carriage; behind her
on a big brown horse, the prince with his hands
tied behind his back.

Beside the prince rode the executioner, his silver sword rattling at his side. And on the

prince's right was the jester, riding on a donkey named Esmerelda.

Sometimes they rode two-by-two, and sometimes four-by-four. Sometimes they whispered or gossiped, and sometimes they rode in silence. But there was always the sound of the horses' hooves and the yelping of the dogs.

As they rode through each town and village of Chelm, people came out of their homes and out of their shops to watch the royal procession. But there were no cheers. The sight of the captive prince riding beside the executioner stirred only sadness among the people.

*B*eside a river, the travelers rested beneath a canopy of trees. The ladies gathered together in a circle, exchanging confidences, mainly about the aches in their noble bottoms. The executioner fell fast asleep by the water. The king and queen sat together holding hands and wondering sadly what would become of the kingdom if the prince were to lose his head after all. And the prince sat beside his friend, the jester.

"Do you really think that the three sages will have an answer?" asked the prince.

"Look how the light dances upon the river water," said the jester.

"Tell me truly," said the prince with a sigh, "can these three men really help me?"

"How very green the grass is along the riverbank this time of year," said the jester. "Isn't it lovely?"

"Dash it all!" said the prince, drawing himself up. "You must tell me. Will these sages be able to help?"

The jester thought for a moment. "I will tell you the truth," he said at last. "It is a case of yes or no. If you were to ask the people of my town, the answer would be 'yes, the three sages are wise enough to help you.' But the people of my town have little need of real wisdom. So the little wisdom that the sages have is more than enough. In your case, we have need of *real* wisdom. So I say to you, 'It is a case of yes or no.'"

"As I thought," said the prince with a sigh. "I must lose my head in the end. And whether here

or there, whether now or later, it makes little difference."

"Oh," said the jester, "here or there makes all the difference in the world. We must all die someday. Nothing lives that does not die. But losing a head now is never as good as losing it later. And losing it here is never as good as losing it there. Most important, you must never lose hope. As long as you have your head, keep it. That is my advice."

"Well," said the prince, looking about, "in that case, the grass really *is* lovely this time of the year, and the sun *does* shine beautifully on the river."

Then the jester sang this song:

> *The king and queen together,*
> *Together, together.*
> *The king and queen together,*
> *And long may they reign.*
>
> *Now come and see the princess,*
> *The princess, the princess.*
> *Now come and see the princess.*
> *She'll make a lovely queen.*

Behold the prince this instant,
This instant, this instant.
Behold the prince this instant,
For soon he will be king.

The sun and moon forever,
Forever, forever.
The sun and moon forever,
They are the king and queen.

The prince smiled gracefully at the jester. "All this," he said, "on account of a silly little egg!"

"Who knows what is silly in the end," asked the jester, "or even what is little? Kings and queens may be little people made large. And eggs may be the largest of things made little."

Soon the royal procession rode on, passing through one town after another. At last the kingdom's end was near. The jester pointed to a forest and said, "My town is just beyond this wood."

The sound of the horses and the dogs brought

the sleepy town to life. Songbirds took flight and chickens scurried here and there. Dogs barked at the invaders and cats clawed up trees. And people appeared at every doorway to see what was causing all the commotion.

Now the jester dug his heels into Esmerelda's sides. The poor donkey brayed and rushed to take the lead. The jester waved to his mom and dad as the procession passed his house. He turned around on Esmerelda's back, pointed to his parents, and yelled to the prince, "That's my sun, and that's my moon!" And all the lords and ladies of the court waved to the jester's mom and dad—except the prince, whose hands were tied behind his back.

CHAPTER SIX

True Wisdom Revealed

The three sages were eating lunch when the parade came to a halt at their door. Blossom looked out the window to see where all the noise was coming from. When she saw the king and queen, the lords and all the ladies, she thought, "It's just like the tales in the book—and it's all come true at last." She ran and removed the plates from the table, snatching the food away from the sages even as they were raising forks to their lips. Blossom cleared everything off the table, combed the sages' hair, and dusted their beards. Then she opened the door.

In came the king, dressed in his robes of velvet and silver, all braided in gold. In came the queen in her gown of ermine and cape of sable. In came the jester in his silks of green and red, his shoes of yellow that curled at the toes, and his comical hat. In came the sword-bearing executioner, leading a handsome young man with head bowed and hands tied behind his back.

At that moment, something happened to Blossom that had never happened before. She wrinkled her brow. She put her hand to her mouth and muffled a cry of "Aha!" And she stared at the prince and began to ponder his troubles.

No one paid any attention to Blossom. Every eye was turned toward the three sages sitting at the table. The lords and the ladies of the court all crowded into the small room, filling it with their colorful silks and satins, scenting the air with rare and fragrant perfumes.

Slowly, the sages rose to their feet and bowed to the king. "Welcome, Your Majesty," said the first sage. "Welcome, welcome," said the second sage. "Welcome, welcome, welcome all!" added the third.

"We have come from afar to seek your wisdom," said the king. "It is said that you are the wisest three sages in all the kingdom of Chelm. They tell me that only you can save the life of the prince, my son."

The three sages sat down and folded their hands on the table and waited for the king to continue. This was how they always sat when someone came to ask for wisdom. How could they know that when a king is present, only the king is allowed to sit?

The gentlemen and the ladies of the court whispered to one another, embarrassed to see the sages sitting while the king still stood. But the king paid no attention. He proceeded to tell his story.

"There were only five eggs on the platter," he said. "I asked for six. I asked for them whole, and I asked for them fast. But when they arrived, one was missing."

The king went on. "The jester had eaten the egg. So I ordered that his head be cut off. That is the punishment when a man cannot pay his debt to the king. And what was the debt of the jester? Not just an egg, but an egg that could have hatched a chicken, and a chicken that might have laid many eggs, many eggs that might have made many chickens—a thousand and one chickens—and not one less!

"But just as the jester's head was about to be removed from his shoulders, the prince said, 'Wait. It was my fault, not the jester's, for I dropped the egg, making it unfit for a king to eat.' Once a royal judgment is given, it *must* be carried out. And, since it was the prince's fault—as all know is true—the prince's head must go."

The king sat down upon a chair beside the fireplace and said, "Now, I ask you three sages, what possible answer can there be? Is there some way to spare my son and honor my law as well?"

As you might expect, the first sage furrowed his forehead, knotted his brow, wrinkled the skin of his face, and clenched his fists on the table. How wise he appeared, how deep and profound seemed his thoughts! The ladies and gentlemen of the court "oohed" and "ahed."

Not to be outdone, the second sage jumped to his feet, stuck a finger prominently in the air, opened his eyes as wide as they would open, and exclaimed, "Aha!" Then, again, in the loudest

voice he had ever used, "Aha!" And yet again—
his cry splitting the air as a woodsman splits a
log—"AHA!"

This was followed by many more "aha"s,
some of which sounded like "aha?" and some of
which sounded like "ah-ha" and some of which
sounded like "ahaha, ahaha."

"He has an idea," agreed several gentlemen of
the court, waiting patiently to hear what the second sage would say. But all he said was that
one word.

The third sage looked at his two friends and
shook his head. "No, no," he insisted, "those
ideas will never do." Then he turned to the king
and the queen, to the executioner and the prince
and the jester, to the lords and the ladies, and he
said, "Let there be silence. I'm ready to ponder."

Silence spread over everyone and everything
in the room—a stillness such as had not been
heard since the moment before God created the
world. Not a breath could be heard as the third
sage set his eyes upon the table and began to
ponder. He pondered the tabletop until he saw a
place where the wood was scratched. He pon-

dered the scratch until he saw where the scratch ended in a dot. He pondered the dot until he fell fast asleep.

Then he began to snore.

"Oh, dear me," said the queen. She swooned and would have fallen to the floor if the jester and the executioner had not caught her. Blossom ran to fetch two pails of water. One was poured on the queen's hands, and one on her head. At last, she opened her eyes.

"Did I miss anything?" she asked the executioner.

He shook his head. "I don't think so," he said.

The sage of the knitted brow still sat with his brow tightly lined. The sage of "Aha!" still murmured softly. And the sage of ponder snored ponderously.

No one could imagine what would happen next.

Then, as sudden as a thunderstorm in summer, the king sat up in his chair and began to laugh. He stood up and walked to the sage of the knitted brow, looked closely, and laughed again. He put his ear to the mouth of the second sage, heard a faint "aha," and laughed even harder. He stopped only long enough to wipe the tears of joy from his eyes and put his hand on the sage of ponder, who was still snoring. The king broke out in a new gale of laughter more mighty than the last.

Watching her husband set the queen to giggling. She could hardly keep her nose in the air. The laughter woke the pondering sage, who immediately began to ponder its cause. Then the laughter seized the ladies and the gentlemen of the court. No sooner did they wipe away the tears with their silk handkerchiefs then new tears appeared in their place. Unable to stand steady on their feet, the royal court tripped and fell one upon another, crying and laughing, laughing and crying.

The queen rolled over four gentlemen and fell flat on her back, trying to say, "I *(giggle)* must *(ouch!)* learn *(oops!)* to *(yipe!)* be *(oy!)* more *(giggle)* careful."

The king landed in a heap on the chair by the fireplace, his belly heaving until he could laugh no more. His crown tilted on his head. His robes

twisted. He leaned back in the chair, weeping tears half of joy and half of sadness.

In the center of all the toppling and rolling stood the jester and the prince, neither of them amused.

And, in the corner of the room, still holding a pail half-filled with water, stood Blossom. She was not laughing, either. Not even smiling a bit.

The king slowly gathered his wits. The sound of chuckling slowly thinned and cleared. The ladies and gentlemen of the court wiped their eyes one last time, sat up straight in their places on the floor, and held their sides in pain. The queen picked herself up, dusted off her furs, and raised her nose to its familiar pose.

"THEY CALL THEMSELVES SAGES!" thundered the king. "There are better sages in my henhouse! Wiser men tend my garden. Why, there is not an ounce of sense in these three 'wise' minds combined! Sages, indeed!"

That's the most ungrateful thing I have ever heard," said Blossom, pointing an accusing finger at the king. "You are a terrible person to talk that way. Why, you are the very one who created this mess. You know full well that you could have eaten five eggs instead of six and that belly of yours would have been satisfied. But no! You want to cut off a head in exchange for an egg! Do you think *that* is wise?"

The gentlemen and the ladies of the court covered their faces in terror. No one—not even the queen—had ever spoken to the king in such a manner. Surely this girl's head would shortly be removed from her fair neck. The executioner checked the sharpness of his sword.

Blossom showed no fear. She reached behind the prince and untied his hands. Then she faced the king again. "You have come all this way for an answer—though, heaven knows, the answer was before you all the time. But, since you have come for an answer, I shall give it to you."

Blossom went to the stove, where the food was still warming, and dipped a spoon into one of the pots. Then she brought the spoon to the prince and said, "Give that to the king, and your debt will be paid in full."

The prince looked at the spoon in his hand.

"There is nothing here but one boiled pea!" he said.

Blossom smiled. "From one pea comes a pea plant, and from one pea plant come many peas, and from many peas come many vines, and so on forever. So give that to the king, and let him plant it."

The jester began to smile as Blossom continued: "There is one problem, of course. From a boiled pea no vine can grow. A boiled pea is good only for eating. And, as everyone knows, as even the wise citizens of Chelm must admit, from a boiled egg no chicken can hatch. A boiled egg is good only for eating!"

The queen looked at her husband. "She's right, you know."

Then the king rose to his feet. He shifted his weight back and forth for a moment, then replied to his wife. "I knew it all along," he said, straightening the crown on his head. "I just wanted to know if wisdom truly could be found anywhere in the realm of Chelm. And now, I think I've found it at last."

"Oh," said the ladies of the court, nodding in agreement. "Here, here," said the gentlemen of the court, smiling.

"Wasn't it a lovely journey?" asked the king. "And won't we all have fun on the ride back?"

CHAPTER SEVEN

Ever After

Blossom's mother soon learned that her daughter had spoken the truth fearlessly to the king. Now Becky understood why Blossom had always seemed so special. She said, "All along, my daughter has been like a rose. Look how she held herself so tightly closed among the thorns of tears and pain. Look how she waited patiently all these years, as a rose waits for the rain to pass. And see how brightly she opened to reveal her true and inner beauty the moment the rain came to an end. If only I had known that from the beginning, if only I had paid more attention to the lovely little rosebud than I had to the thorns, I would never have had to leave home at all!" Amy and Deb agreed. And Jake just smiled. He had always seen the rose inside the bud. He had always known that Blossom would one day blossom.

The prince had also taken a good look at Blossom. And he very much liked what he saw. Not only was she wise, she was beautiful as well. Her raven-black hair and her lily-white skin, her sapphire-blue eyes and her delicately rose-colored cheeks—everything about her was perfect, he thought. Even the proud way she walked with her nose held slightly in the air. He thanked Blossom for saving his life, and he married her, making her his princess.

The king invited the three sages to live in the palace as his teachers, for in Chelm it is said, "No one is ever so wise as one who is sometimes silly." He took lessons in knitting his brow, learned to say a passable "Aha!" and was tutored in "The Finer Points of Ponder." The Master of Ponder declared the king his finest student ever.

Many years later, when the prince became king, Blossom became queen. But she never forgot the names of all the trees of the forest, all the mushrooms that were good to eat, and all the stories of kings and queens, princes and princesses that she had read as a child.